Miyu
and the
Cranes for Peace

by Alexandra Behr

illustrations by Oki Han

 HOUGHTON MIFFLIN   BOSTON

My name is Miyu (MEE-yoo). I live in San Francisco, California.

San Francisco is famous for its steep hills, cable cars, the Golden Gate Bridge, and the most crooked street in the world. San Francisco is where many people from different cultures live, including Japanese Americans, like my family.

The first Japanese moved here in the early 1860s. In 1906, a huge earthquake caused fires that destroyed much of the city. Many people lost their homes. Japanese American families moved to an area called Japantown. They opened restaurants, built churches and shrines, and ran shops.

Today my parents are part of the Japantown tradition. They own a stationery store in the center of Japantown. They sell paper goods and writing supplies.

My parents were born in Osaka, Japan, but I was born in San Francisco. My mom likes to tell me about growing up in Osaka.

She told me that when she was young, she lived in an apartment in Osaka with her parents and brother. She wore a red backpack to school, like the other girls. Her brother wore a black backpack, like the other boys.

My mom and her friends held hands when they walked to and from school. Whenever it rained after school, they ran for cover under a store awning.

When the rain stopped, the children went home for afternoon snacks. My mom often ate a piece of cake or rice crackers. She always drank green tea with her snack.

After her snack, my mom played outside with her friends. She liked to jump rope, just like I do. She liked to play hide and seek too.

My mom had three pets: a cat, a rabbit, and a goldfish.

"We had to be careful that our cat did not go fishing in the goldfish bowl!" she told me.

Every year on March 3, my mom celebrated *Hina Matsuri* (HEE-nah Maht-SOOR-ee), or the Dolls' Festival. On that day, Japanese girls set special dolls on shelves covered with red cloth. My mom had fifteen dolls, including the rulers of Japan, royal ladies, and musicians. The dolls had tiny furniture and food.

My mom's friends came to her home. They looked at the dolls, ate rice cakes, and sang songs. Then my mom went to her friends' homes to look at their dolls.

I asked my mom what she liked to eat for dinner. "Spaghetti and hamburgers," she said.

I like to eat those foods too!

She also ate Japanese curry, made of beef, carrots, and other vegetables. They ate it with rice. Now my mom makes curry for us. I help her cook by peeling the carrots.

Sometimes I help at my parents' stationery store. They sell paper called *washi* (WA-shee). It is thin and easy to fold. We use washi to make *origami* (o-ree-GAH-mee). Origami means "folded paper."

There are more than 100 traditional origami shapes from Japan. I want to learn how to make them all. I can fold paper frogs, cranes, swans, and spiders. I can also fold paper cups, boxes, hats, and stars!

One week in April, I folded origami cranes for my parents' shop window. I made twenty cranes for good luck. On Saturday Ms. Rollins, my art teacher from school, visited the store. She was in Japantown for the Cherry Blossom Festival.

"Miyu, your cranes are beautiful!" she said. "Can you teach me how to make them?"

"OK," I said. "I'll teach you on Monday."

After my art teacher left, I visited the festival with my friend and her older brother. We watched the Cherry Blossom Festival parade and heard the pounding Japanese drums. We saw karate experts kick and punch. We watched dance performers. We visited flower arranging exhibitions and tea ceremonies. Then we stopped by a snack booth and ate rice cakes.

On Monday, I brought washi paper to school. Before art class, I showed Ms. Rollins how to fold the square pieces of paper. We made a dog, a cat, and a crane.

When the other students arrived, my teacher taught them how to make a dog and a cat. They're easy to fold. Then she taught them how to make a crane. Cranes are harder to make because they have many folds. When we were done, we placed our origami on a bookshelf.

The next day, my mom visited our art class. She wore a *kimono* (kuh-MOH-noh), which is a long robe tied with a belt.

"I like your origami animals," she said. "Origami has a special role in Japan. The Children's Peace Monument is in Hiroshima, Japan. The monument was built after World War II. Now children from all over the world send origami cranes to the Children's Peace Monument. Cranes stand for peace as well as good luck."

"Who wants to send origami cranes to Hiroshima?" Ms. Rollins asked.

Everyone did!

My mom had brought a lot of washi paper to class. She handed out the paper to the students. Each student made five cranes. We used string to tie them together. Then we wrote a letter to send with the cranes.

We mailed the box with the letter and cranes to the Children's Peace Monument.

Madison School, Room 12
San Francisco, CA
April 17, 2003

Dear Hiroshima Peace Culture Foundation,

Our teacher and our classmate Miyu taught us how to make paper cranes. Miyu's mother is from Japan. She told us that origami cranes stand for peace. Please hang these cranes on the Children's Peace Monument. We hope the world will live in peace one day.

Sincerely,
Ms. Rollins's Class

This summer I rode on a plane to Osaka, Japan. My parents and I visited my cousins. Then we took a train to Hiroshima.

In Hiroshima, we went to the Children's Peace Monument. I walked around and around the monument. There were many, many cranes from all over the world. Among them, I found the cranes we had made in class.

I placed on the monument one more string of cranes that I had made. And I made a wish for peace.

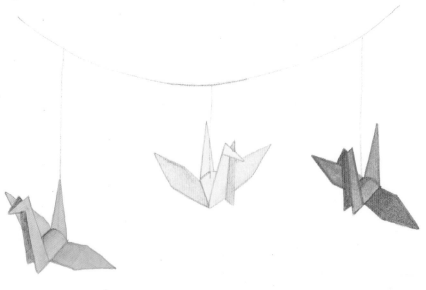